CONTENTS

KIDNAP AT
DENTON FARM

CHAPTER 1

A STORM IN A TEASET

"Wow – look at that!" Shaz and Mickey stood with their heads tilted back, watching the wind turbine's three great blades rotate at the top of its gleaming white tower. "How high is it?"

"Forty metres," grinned Titch. "You can see it from miles away."

Mickey nodded. "I bet you can. I wondered what was going on when I saw those trucks arriving with the parts. They got it up quick, didn't they?"

"Two days," said Jillo, "once they had the base laid. It'll make all the electricity Mum and Dad need to run the farm, but I'm afraid it's causing a bit of trouble."

"What sort of trouble?" asked Shaz. "I thought everybody was in favour of wind power – clean, renewable and all that."

"Well, yes, that's what they say, but Dad reckons you can never please everybody. Some people in the village are saying it interferes with the telly. Others don't like the noise, and some say it's ugly – spoils the view."

"It's better than pylons," said Mickey. "They really are ugly, but nobody mentions them."

"It beats nuclear power stations, too," put in Shaz. "My grandad says nuclear power's poisonous."

"Well, anyway, there's trouble," said Jillo. "There were two letters in last night's paper, and Reuben Kilchaffinch is starting a protest group."

"Huh!" scoffed Shaz. "Reuben Kilchaffinch would, wouldn't he? He's a professional troublemaker. Anyway, his dilapidated farm spoils the view far more than any turbine could."

"It's just 'cause it's something new," said Mickey. "It'll die down when people get used to it. It's a storm in a teaset."

"Teacup, you div!" laughed Titch.

"Huh?"

"It's a teacup, Mickey, not a teaset. Who brought you up?"

"I brought myself up, didn't I?"

Mickey's mum had left when he was very small, and his dad was away a lot, so Mickey lived with Raider the dog in a caravan at the edge of Weeping Wood.

"I suppose you did," conceded Titch, "so I'll let you off."

"Thanks a lot," growled Mickey.

"D'you think there's a job here for The Outfit?" asked Shaz. "Watching this protest group for instance." The Outfit was the name of their gang. The only members were the four of them and Raider.

"Shouldn't think so," said Mickey. "They're not going to try blowing the turbine up or anything. They'll march around with banners or something. Hand out leaflets. Get up a petition." He grinned. "We can watch 'em if you like – it'll give us something to do." It was the Spring holidays, and they needed something to do.

"I vote we return to HQ and make a plan," said Titch, so they did.

9

CHAPTER 2

BADGES

HQ was a large hut in the corner of one of Farmer Denton's fields. The Dentons were Titch and Jillo's parents. They'd given the hut to The Outfit. On the door was a notice: HQ THE OUTFIT – No Admittance. Inside was a table and six chairs. There was an iron stove too, with a saucepan and a kettle on it. The walls were covered with maps and pictures, and there was a rug on the floor. Raider's basket stood near the stove.

"Right," said Mickey, when they were all seated. Raider sat on the chair next to Mickey's, his forepaws on the table. He was a lurcher, but he liked to pretend to be human. "You suggested this meeting, Titch, so you start." At seven, Titch was the youngest member of The Outfit.

"Well," she said, "for a start, there'll be no need to be out in the middle of the night this time."

"Why not?" asked Shaz. His parents were on a long visit to Pakistan, so it was fairly easy for him to get out at night.

"Because Jillo and I can see the turbine from our bedroom window. If anybody tries to interfere with it at night, we'll raise the alarm and Dad can deal with 'em."

"Huh," grumbled Mickey, who sometimes spent all night outside when his dad was away. "Takes away half the fun, that."

"It makes it easier for me and Titch though," said Jillo. "You know how hard it is for us to get out after dark."

"Okay," nodded Mickey. "So what do we do, folks?"

"Well," continued Titch. "The protest group's holding a public meeting tomorrow evening at the Village Hall. I think we should be there."

"Would we get in?" asked Shaz. "Kids might not be allowed."

"We can turn up and try," said Titch, "and if they won't let us in we'll make such a racket outside they'll wish they had."

"That sounds like my sort of thing," grinned Mickey.

"I thought we might make a placard to hold up," continued Titch. "It would say 'Wind Power is Clean', or something like that."

"Yes," put in Jillo, "and I've made us some badges. Look." She pulled some cardboard discs from her jeans pocket and laid them out on the table. "They're not just for the meeting – they're Outfit badges. I thought we could wear them all the time, except perhaps when we're at school."

Mickey leaned across, picked up a badge and examined it. "Hey that's pretty nifty, Jillo. I like the way you've fastened the safety pin on the back." He turned it over. "A big nought with a five inside it – what's that mean?"

"It's not a nought," said Jillo, "it's a letter O, for Outfit, and the five's because there are five of us, including Raider. I've made a special one for him – one that'll go on his collar."

"You're a genius," grinned Shaz, pinning his badge on his jacket. "I'm really looking forward to showing up at the meeting with this on so everybody knows who we are."

"Right." Mickey's badge was in place, and he was busy attaching Raider's to his collar. "The Outfit's ready for action like never before. Let's do the oath."

They squatted in a circle with Raider in the middle and chanted:

"Faithful, fearless, full of fun,
Winter, summer, rain or sun,
One for five and five for one –
THE OUTFIT!"

They shouted the last line and sprang upright,

arms raised high. "Woof!" went Raider, and they broke the circle, laughing.

CHAPTER 3

NO SPIES

The meeting was set for half past seven. Mickey, Shaz, Jillo and Titch arrived at the Village Hall at twenty-five past, wearing their badges. Raider wasn't with them. There seemed to be quite a few people going in.

"Looks like Mum and Dad have made a lot of enemies," said Jillo gloomily.

"Not necessarily," said Shaz. "There isn't much to do on a Tuesday night in Lenton. Half these people have probably come for a night out."

Reuben Kilchaffinch was on the door. When he saw the children he scowled. "What in the scrug-busted rumblepoop do you lot want?" he growled.

"We've come to the meeting," said Jillo.

The old farmer peered at her. "You're Len

15

Denton's brat, aren't you? Come to spy, I bet. I'll have no spies at my meeting."

"It's a public meeting," cried Shaz. "Anybody can come."

Reuben shook his head. "Not 'er, nor her sister neither. You two lads can go in, if you leave that outside." He pointed to the placard Mickey was holding.

Mickey shook his head. "If we can't all go in, none of us goes. One for five and five for one, that's our motto."

"Aye, well you can stick your motto up your jumper." Reuben had tangled with The Outfit before and come off worst. "On yer way," he growled. "It's half past and I'm shutting this door."

"What now?" asked Titch, gazing at the closed door.

"Now we march," said Mickey. "Round and round the building, and we chant."

"Chant what?" queried Shaz.

"I thought you'd never ask," grinned Mickey. "Listen to this:

We're The Outfit, we all say
Denton's turbine's here to stay.
Reub can stick his protest group

Up his busted rumblepoop."

"Terrific!" laughed Jillo. "Let's go." They formed a line and set off round the building. Mickey held up the placard. The Wind is Green, it said. The chant was a bit ragged because they kept laughing, but they didn't care. After a while somebody inside started slamming windows.

"Reuben can't hear himself think," chuckled Shaz.

"You can't hear what isn't there," rejoined Jillo, and they marched on, reeling with mirth.

The meeting broke up at nine o'clock. When people started coming out of the hall the children stood in a row beside the path, holding up the banner. Some people ignored it; others read it as they passed. Presently they saw Linda Fellgate approaching. Linda was a reporter on the local paper.

"Excuse me," said Jillo.

"Yes?" The reporter paused.

"Can you tell us what happened in the meeting, please? They wouldn't let us in."

"Oh, well, the Chairman – that's Mr Kilchaffinch – explained to the meeting what

17

he and his friends have against the turbine and appealed for people to join them. There are only six of them so far and they called themselves LAWP – that's Lenton Against Wind Power. They aim to get a thousand signatures on a petition to the council, and they're urging people to write to their MP. They need funds to print leaflets. They hope to organize a march and a sit-in in the near future." She smiled. "That's about it so far."

"Will you be putting it in the paper?" asked Titch.

"Oh, yes. There'll be a full report in tomorrow's edition, plus a picture." She grinned. "This is the biggest thing that's happened in Lenton since the baker's van had a puncture. See you, kids!"

Walking home, Mickey said, "Hey – I wonder if Ms Fellgate'll mention us in the paper?"

Shaz shook his head. "Shouldn't think so, but we can buy a copy and look, can't we? At least we'll get a photo of old Reuben to pin on the wall."

"Oh, wow!" squealed Jillo. "I can't wait."

CHAPTER 4
POSTIE

They watched the turbine all the next day, but LAWP never came near. Finally, at three o'clock Jillo said, "The paper'll be out now – who's off down to get one?"

It was a very warm day and nobody seemed keen so she went herself. There it was on the front page: Linda Fellgate's report of the meeting under a photo of Reuben Kilchaffinch and what looked like a roomful of people.

"The picture's a swizz," she told herself. "There weren't that many people there." She sat on a bench in the park and read the report. Right at the bottom Linda Fellgate had written:

Throughout the meeting a group of children staged a noisy demonstration outside the hall

19

in support of the turbine. Among them were Jill and Matilda Denton, the daughters of the turbine's owner.

"Oh, heck!" Jillo pulled a face. "There'll be trouble when Dad sees that. He said it was best to ignore the meeting."

She was folding the paper ready to set off back when a gruff voice she recognized said, "Got your name in the paper, I see."

She looked up smiling. "Hello, Postie. Yes, it's fame at last."

Postie had been the village postman until his retirement a few years ago. He shopped in Lenton nearly every day and always had a cheery word for those he met. His real name was Albert but everybody called him Postie. Jillo liked him.

"Aye," he chuckled. "Fame, and you didn't have to wait till retirement day like I did, neither. Sixty-five I was, before I got my name in the paper."

Jillo smiled. "Never mind, Postie – you're the best known character in Lenton. You don't need publicity."

The old man nodded. "You're probably right, love. I only hope this contraption of your father's doesn't bring trouble, that's all."

"Oh no, Postie," cried Jillo. "Why should it, just because a few cranks object? They'll get used to it."

"Aye, they very likely will. Mind you," he shook his head, "it's a funny thing, the wind. Pigs can see it, y'know."

"Can they?" Jillo was astonished. "I thought it was invisible. In fact we did this poem at school: Who has seen the wind, neither you nor I, but when the trees-di-da di-da-the wind is passing by. I've forgotten a bit of it."

Postie cackled. "By gaw, we had that poem when I was at school, lass. Some things never change, but poets don't know everything, and wind can be funny stuff. I'll see you later."

Jillo watched the old man till he passed from sight round a bend, then sighed. He's losing his marbles, old Postie, she thought. Pigs can see the wind! She grinned. Wait till I tell the others.

CHAPTER 5

GROUNDED

"Is that what he said?" chuckled Mickey. "Pigs can see the wind?"

Jillo nodded. "Poor old guy."

"It might be true," protested Titch. "How do you know what pigs can see?"

"It's a tale," grinned Shaz. "Even I know that, and pigs aren't exactly a Number One topic with me. Anyway." He finished cutting out Linda Fellgate's story and held it up. "Who's got the drawing pins?"

They pinned the article to the wall and sat looking at it. It was nearly five o'clock. "I don't think anything's going to happen before tea," said Mickey. "I vote we go home now, and meet back here at half-six."

"Hmmmm." Jillo pulled a face. "If Dad's in a bad mood about us going to that meeting,

Titch and I might not get to go out again today."

"Well, never mind," consoled Shaz. "If that happens, the rest of us will manage, and you can keep watch from your room."

They locked the hut and split up. Mickey and Raider headed for the caravan, Shaz went towards the village and the two girls set off along the track that led to the farm. No sooner were they through the kitchen door than their father appeared, brandishing a copy of the *Echo*.

"I've just read something quite incredible," he said. He spoke quietly, but Jillo could tell he was terribly angry. "It says here that the two of you demonstrated near the Village Hall last night while Mr Kilchaffinch's meeting was in progress. Tell me it isn't true."

Jillo looked down, biting her lip.

Her father glared at her. "Well?"

"It-it is true, Dad. We were there. We wanted to speak in favour of the turbine but old – but Mr Kilchaffinch wouldn't let us in."

"So you made a din outside?"

"Yes, Dad."

"After I told you the best thing to do was to ignore the whole thing?"

Jillo nodded. "Yes, Dad."

"Well, at least you've been honest about it, but I'm afraid that's not enough. You'll go to your room now and remain there for the rest of the week. You're grounded till school starts again. Good night, Jill."

"But, Dad—"

"No buts. You're grounded and that's that." He turned to Titch. "You went along with your sister because you're not old enough to think for yourself. You will go to bed without supper and that's all. Good night, Matilda."

"I can think!" flared Titch. "I didn't go because of her – I went 'cause I wanted to."

Her father nodded. "Very well, Matilda – you're grounded, too. Off you go now."

"What did you do that for?" demanded Jillo, as soon as they were in their room. "You could've been out tomorrow. You could've told the others what happened. Now they won't know why we don't show up."

"They'll guess," growled Titch. "They might even phone. Anyway, I wasn't going to let Dad tell me I can't think." She gazed through the window. Two fields away, the turbine's blades flashed sunlight as they turned. "They'll have to manage without us, that's all."

Oh, no they won't! Jillo thought but didn't say. Not when there's a handy drainpipe right outside that window. An hour or two to let you fall asleep, little sister, and I'm out of here!

CHAPTER 6

AN EVENING STROLL

Titch fell asleep at half past seven. Jillo spent about five minutes arranging some cushions and soft toys under her duvet to make it look as though she, too, was in bed. It wouldn't fool anyone who came into the room, but if it was dark and Mum just stuck her head round the door as she sometimes did, it might just work.

Getting the window up wasn't easy. It was an old-fashioned sash affair which would open ten centimetres, then jam. To raise it further you had to wiggle it about and that made a noise. Jillo eased it up bit by bit, watching her sister's head on the pillow and listening for footfalls on the stairs. Titch stirred a couple of times but didn't wake, and nobody came to investigate.

The drainpipe route was easy. Jillo had used

it before, though only for a lark – this was her first serious escape. It was eight o'clock when she grabbed the pipe, slid off the sill and swarmed down, dislodging flakes of rust which sifted down the neck of her T-shirt or settled in her hair.

The sun had disappeared behind the barn but hadn't quite set, so it was still light. She crouched at the foot of the pipe, listening. She could hear the TV in the living room, the wind in the sycamores and nothing else.

Crossing the yard on tiptoe, Jillo slipped through the gateway on to the footpath which crossed the fields. She was now hidden from the house by the line of sycamores her great-grandfather had planted as a windbreak. She breathed a sigh of relief and set off towards the hut as the sun's rim touched the horizon.

She was squeezing through the stile in the wall which separated the first field from the twenty-acre, when the man appeared. He'd been lurking in the shadow of the hawthorn which grew beside the wall here, and he stepped out as Jillo cleared the stile.

"Good evening." Jillo started violently and stopped dead. He was a man of medium height, dressed all in black. A balaclava covered his head.

There were two eyeholes in it but no hole for the mouth, so that his voice was muffled. She backed up, groping for the stile with her hands.

"Don't be afraid," said the muffled voice. "I won't hurt you if you do as I say."

"Wh – what d'you want?" stammered Jillo. "I haven't got any money."

The man chuckled. "I don't want money. You'll come with me quietly to a place I've prepared, and there you'll stay till my work is done."

"What place? What work? I don't understand." Jillo wished she was back in the house with Titch. She considered shouting for help, but the man had chosen his spot well. The stile was exactly halfway between the house and the hut. She might yell herself blue in the face and not be heard.

The man stepped forward and took her arm. "You will walk beside me," he insisted, "quietly, as though the two of us were out for an evening stroll. Our direction will be south-east, towards the wood."

Jillo tried to free her arm but the man's grip tightened painfully till she stopped struggling. "People don't usually wear masks," she snarled, "when they're out for an evening stroll."

The man laughed briefly. "Since we're not likely to be seen, that's not important. Come now – the sun's gone, and I want us to complete our walk before dark."

They walked in the twilight, arm in arm like an old married couple. Jillo cried softly all the way, half convinced she'd never see the sun again.

CHAPTER 7

GRAFFITI TIME

"Well," Shaz looked at his watch. "We said half-six and it's nearly half-eight. They won't come now, Mickey."

Mickey sighed. "I know. We shouldn't have let 'em come to the Village Hall last night. We knew they'd be in trouble if it got out."

"We didn't force them," said Shaz. "They came because we're The Outfit and we stick together. They won't be blaming us."

"I know. I just hope – what's that?"

"Sounds like singing. Hang on." Shaz got up and peered through the window. It was getting dark. The colours had gone from the landscape and the turbine was a silhouette against the darkening sky. Somewhere between the turbine and the hut some points of light were moving. Shaz screwed up his eyes and saw a procession of shadowy figures. He turned.

"It's them!" he hissed. "Old Kilchaffinch and his mob. They're coming up the path with lights of some sort. What do we do?"

Mickey joined his friend at the window. "I dunno. It's probably a peaceful protest, Shaz. People have a right to protest, providing they don't do damage. We'll creep up – keep an eye on 'em. If they leave the turbine alone, we'll leave them alone."

The hardest part was keeping Raider quiet. Once he'd got the message the rest was easy. They didn't even need stealth. The protesters' singing drowned out the sounds they made as they crept across the field and crouched in the shadow of the wall.

There were eleven protesters, each carrying a jam jar in which a candle burned. They began circling the base of the turbine in a sort of dance, singing and swaying. The sight of Reuben Kilchaffinch capering on his bandy old legs sent Shaz into a fit of giggles, and Mickey had to nip him really hard to shut him up. Raider, who couldn't see over the wall, sat patiently at his master's feet, hoping there'd be action by and by.

He was not to be disappointed. The two boys had just decided that nothing important was going to happen when Reuben held up a hand. The circling stopped. The singing tailed off. His followers watched in silence as the old farmer produced a spray can from inside his ancient jacket and approached the turbine's base.

"It's graffiti time," murmured Shaz.

"It's not, you know," hissed Mickey. "Raider!" At the sound of the boy's voice the protesters whirled and the dog sprang eagerly to its feet. "Go get 'em, boy – see 'em off!"

It was like a scene in a speeded-up film. As Raider cleared the wall, yapping and snarling in his best imitation of a mad wolf, the protesters threw down their jars and fled. Cursing and swearing, Reuben Kilchaffinch hobbled after them, lashing out at Raider with the spray can as the dog snapped and snarled at his heels. The two boys laughed so much they had to cling to the wall to keep from falling over, and by the time Mickey found enough breath to call Raider off, his victims were 500 metres away and still running.

"Good boy, Raider!" Mickey bent and

ruffled the dog's ears as the three made their way back to the hut. "It'll be a while before they come singing and dancing up here again."

"Yip," agreed Raider, and the two boys laughed. They'd have laughed on the other side of their faces if they'd known what was happening to Jillo at that moment.

CHAPTER 8

A REGULAR LITTLE PALACE

"Right, young woman – in you go." They'd walked through Weeping Wood and out the far side to the old canal, following its overgrown towpath away from Lenton into territory that was unfamiliar to Jillo. It had been dark for some time when they came to a high brick wall which paralleled the towpath. Old trees grew beyond this wall, and halfway along there was a gateway, whose crumbling posts were clad with ivy or some other creeping plant. The masked man had steered her between the posts and up a long-neglected driveway to a great, tall house that nobody had lived in for a long, long time. They'd ascended some slimy steps to the front door which the man had pushed open, propelling Jillo through a pitch-black hallway and up two flights of creaking stairs.

A Regular Little Palace

The room she now found herself in was a poky attic with a small window in its sloping ceiling. A little moonlight penetrated the window's coating of dirt, revealing a spindly wooden chair, a rusty iron fireplace in one wall and a mattress on the floor. On the mattress, folded, were two blankets. There was nothing else. She turned to her abductor.

"Why have you brought me here? I've never harmed you. I want to go home."

The man shook his head. "As I said before, you will stay here till my work is done."

"But there's no light." Jillo was trying to be brave but the words came out as a whimper. "Nothing to eat or drink. It's cold as ice in here, and what am I supposed to do about a loo?"

"All that is taken care of," the man told her. "There'll be food tomorrow, and something to drink, and of course there'll be light through the window during the day. It's like a luxury penthouse suite, this place – a regular little palace. Sleep tight." He backed quickly out of the attic and closed the door.

Jillo heard the scrape of a key in a rusty lock. "I'll scream," she cried. "I'll smash the window and scream my head off till somebody comes and you'll go to prison for ever!"

From beyond the door came a harsh laugh. "Smash the window if you like," said the man. "You'll be cold then all right, and wet when it rains. And as far as screaming, all that'll get you is a sore throat. Good night."

She listened as his footfalls receded, then she seized the brass knob and rattled the door, but it was securely fastened. She stood on tiptoe and tried to see through the window but all it showed her was the moon, so she sank on to the mattress, buried her face in her hands and cried.

CHAPTER 9

MOoNLIGHT

It was eleven-thirty when Titch, asleep since half past seven, woke and called out sleepily to her sister. She'd dreamed she was tied to the blades of the turbine which revolved slowly, while far below Reuben Kilchaffinch and thousands of pigs gazed up at her.

Getting no reply, she called more sharply, with the same result. It wasn't that the dream had frightened her. On the contrary, it was quite amusing and Titch wanted to tell Jillo about it. Besides, she didn't see why her sister should sleep soundly while she herself lay awake.

She got out of bed, crossed the strip of carpet and reached for Jillo's shoulder. Her hand closed round something unfamiliar which moved in an unconvincing way when she shook it. Peeling back the duvet, she found herself gazing at Teddy Redkecks, boon companion of her toddlerhood.

Titch's first instinct was to yell for her parents. Jillo's bed had obviously been rigged to make it look occupied, so her sister wasn't in the bathroom or downstairs raiding the fridge. The clock on the bedside cabinet said eleven thirty-one, so even if she'd shinned down the pipe and gone off to meet the others, she'd surely have been back before now.

Titch went over to the window, lifted the curtain and looked out. Moonlight dappled the garden, making the fields look silver, and flashed rhythmically off the turbine's revolving blades. Nothing stirred on the ground – the Friesians in the first field stood like statues on the silvery grass. She let the curtain fall.

What shall I do? She sat down on her bed. If I get Mum and Dad and Jillo's out there somewhere with the boys, she'll be in awful trouble when she comes home. How long should I wait for her to show up? Suppose she's not with Shaz and Mickey? What if she's been knocked down by a car or she's lying somewhere with a broken leg? I've got to tell Mum and Dad, haven't I? There's worse things than being in bother with your parents.

She got up and padded barefoot along the landing and down the stairs. The TV was on in the living room. She pushed open the door. Her father looked round, saw the expression on her face and stood up.

"What is it, Matilda? Are you ill?"

Titch shook her head. Mum got up and came towards her.

"Then what is it, darling? Did you have a dream?"

"No. Well – yes, but that's not it, Mum. Jillo's not in her bed. She's not in the house. She's gone."

CHAPTER 10

SOMETHING MORE IMPORTANT

Mickey woke with a start as Raider yipped. "Wassamarra, you daft mutt?" he mumbled, peering at the clock on the bedside table. 00.09. "Nine minutes past midnight, and you hear a flippin' rabbit or something. Go back to sleep."

He turned over and closed his eyes, but Raider had got up and was growling by the door. Mickey sighed and sat up. "What is it, boy?"

"Yip!"

"Someone out there, you reckon?"

"Yip!"

"Oh, all right." He rolled out of bed, took his dad's shotgun from its hooks on the wall and crossed to the door. When he lifted the curtain there was enough moonlight to show him a man coming out of the trees. As the man approached the caravan, Mickey was surprised to recognize Mr Denton.

What's he want after midnight? he wondered. Maybe he's come to tell me off for taking Titch and Jillo down the Village Hall. Funny time to choose, though. Anyway, I won't need this. He laid the gun aside, unlocked the door and opened it. "Mr Denton?"

"Mickey – is Jill with you?"

"Huh – no, Mr Denton, she's not. Isn't she at home?"

"Obviously not or I wouldn't be here, would I?" snapped the farmer. "Did you see her at any time this evening?"

Mickey shook his head. "We waited, me and Shaz. At the hut. We waited till half past eight, then we decided she and Ti— she and Matilda must've been grounded."

The farmer nodded. "They were, but sometime between seven-thirty and eleven-thirty Jill left the house, and I thought she might have come to you. I'd better get back now – call the police."

Mickey nodded. "Me and Raider'll take a look around, Mr Denton – see what we can find."

The farmer, halfway to the trees already, nodded. "You do that, Mickey. Thanks." He strode off.

Mickey pulled on some clothes. "C'mon, Raider," he murmured. "We've something more important than rabbits to sniff out tonight."

They quartered the silvery fields, concentrating on the shadowy sides of walls and hedgerows. From time to time Mickey stopped and called, but there was no response. They searched for thirty minutes, then Raider picked up a scent by the stile in the twenty-acre and went yipping towards the wood.

"Rabbit," muttered Mickey. "Raider!" he called. "You come back here, boy!" but he might as well have shouted at the moon. "I've noticed a good strong scent sends you deaf, boy," he grumbled, turning away. "I keep meaning to ask the vet about it."

As he crossed the track a police car was coming up from Lenton, its blue light flashing.

CHAPTER 11
ONLY A DOG

Raider was a good dog, but he was only a dog. There was no way he could tell Mickey about the scent he'd found. All he could do when the boy refused to come any further was to follow it by himself.

He did this faithfully, ignoring the most appetizing rabbit scents which criss-crossed it, and it took him right through Weeping Wood, which he knew, and out along the old canal, which he didn't.

Clear of the trees he ran in bright moonlight that glinted on the badge he wore. The badge held a trace of the scent he was following, but being a dog, Raider had no idea why. It was one of the countless small mysteries that made life interesting for him.

He reached the old house a little after 1 a.m.

The scent told him his two friends had gone in by the front door but this was now closed, so he set off round the outside of the house to look for a way in.

There was none. All three doors were securely fastened, and most of the ground-floor windows were boarded up. The house was dark and silent and gave off a smell which was partly a feeling and which made Raider shiver. He couldn't understand why his friends had gone in, and why they didn't come out. When he'd been all the way round he returned to the battered door and pawed at it, whining. Nothing stirred. No light came on.

There was only one thing left to do, and Raider did it. He had a bark that could be heard five kilometres away at night. He barked, listened, barked again. After four volleys of barking he heard a sound like tinkling glass and a voice he knew called faintly from somewhere above his head.

"Raider?" it cried. "Is that you, boy?"

"Yip!"

"Oh, Raider! Fetch Mickey! Go fetch Mickey, boy!"

He didn't understand. His friend sounded so frightened. So sad. Why didn't she come to him? They could run through the wood, over patches of shadow and splashes of moonlight with cool grass under their feet and the breeze in their hair. There'd be rabbits – plenty of rabbits – and somewhere at the end would be Mickey, same as always. Mickey whose name she had called.

He waited, watching the door, but she didn't come. She called a couple of times and he thought she was coming, but she didn't. He was only a dog, so when it had been quiet for a while he forgot why he was waiting. He didn't like it here. He got up and padded off down the tangled driveway, sniffing at tufts and bushes as he went.

CHAPTER 12

NOT THE SAME

There wasn't much the police could do that Wednesday night, but on Thursday morning they were out at first light – sixty of them, combing the countryside. After a while they were joined by a party of volunteers from the village and together they searched all day. Officers made door-to-door inquiries throughout Lenton. The village pond was dragged. So was Froglet Pond, and a short stretch of the canal Raider had passed in the moonlight.

A policewoman picked up Shaz and Mickey and went with them to The Outfit's HQ to see whether Jillo had been there during the night. When she'd gone the pair joined the volunteer searchers, but when the search was suspended at dusk, Jillo was still missing.

Back at HQ, Mickey looked at Shaz. "What are we gonna do?"

Shaz shook his head. "Dunno, but it's not the same without her, is it?"

"No. It feels funny without Titch, too."

"Yeah." Shaz nodded. "Can't expect 'em to let Titch out, though, can you?"

" 'Course not. Shall we light the stove – make a cup of tea?"

"Why not? We could go out again later."

Mickey looked at him. "What time can you stay out till?"

"Eleven. Half past, even. Grandad'll understand if I say we've been searching."

While the two boys were sipping their tea, the phone rang at Denton Farm. The farmer was out, searching his barns and outbuildings by torchlight, so Mrs Denton picked up the phone.

"Lenton 4686." Her voice was hoarse from crying.

"Mrs Denton?"

"Yes, but you're not very clear. Could you speak up, please?"

"Never mind that. I've got your kid. Dismantle the turbine or you'll never see her again."

"What? You've got Jill? Where – where is she? Is she hurt?"

"She's not hurt, but she will be if you don't do as I tell you."

"You're mad! Who are you? If you harm my child I'll— Hello?" The line was dead. She dropped the phone and collapsed weeping on to the sofa.

"We taking Raider?" The boys had finished their tea and were preparing to resume their search.

Mickey shook his head. "No, he'll only go chasing rabbits. We'll drop him off at the van."

They locked up the hut, took the dog to the caravan and set off into the woods with torches, calling Jillo's name. Raider lay by the door and listened to their receding voices – Jillo, Jillo, Jillo! He whined, unable to understand why his hackles rose, why he saw a dark old house and cold white light on water.

CHAPTER 13

RAYS

She was cold – far too cold to sleep. Her blankets were hopelessly thin – one was in holes – and an icy draught filled the attic from the window she'd broken last night. She got up and paced the tiny room, wearing the blankets like a shawl over her clothes.

Her abductor had come stumping up the stairs at half past ten that morning, carrying a plastic bag with sandwiches and a canned fizzy drink. She'd been dying for the loo, and he'd taken her down one flight to a dirty bathroom with a boarded up window.

"Hurry up," he'd mumbled through the balaclava, "and no tricks – I'll be right outside."

She'd used the loo – to her surprise the flush worked – and washed her hands and face in cold water. There was neither soap nor towel.

She'd dried her face on one of the room's ragged curtains and he'd hurried her back up the stairs.

She'd asked for more blankets and he'd laughed. "I told you you'd be cold if you smashed that window, but I see you smashed it anyway so you must take the consequences."

He'd picked up the bits of broken glass while she ate her sandwiches, piling them in the empty grate so that she abandoned her second request – that she might have a bit of a fire. Not that she'd expected him to agree anyway – a smoking chimney in a supposedly empty house would be a bit of a giveaway.

He'd waited while she finished the fizzy drink then, at her request, had taken the can down to the bathroom, filled it with water and brought it back to her. This small act of consideration had encouraged her and she'd asked. "Why am I here? What is this work you have to do?"

He laughed harshly inside his mask. "I have to stop the rays, of course."

"Rays? What rays? What d'you mean?"

Another laugh. "Don't pretend you don't know or I might get angry, and you wouldn't like that. The rays from the turbine, of course.

The ones your father zaps me
head's ready to explode and I can't thin.

"There are—" She'd been about to sa
there are no rays – you must be mad, but she
stopped herself, because a little voice inside
her head warned, be careful – he is mad, but it
wouldn't be a good idea to tell him so. Instead
she whispered, "Oh, I see. Those rays. How
will you stop them?"

A chuckle. "Simple. I force 'em to dismantle
the turbine. When that's done, they get you back.

"But – Dad won't dismantle the turbine. It
cost thousands of pounds."

"Of course it did – that's the ray gun, you
see – but he'll take it down to save your life."

"My – my life?"

"Oh, yes. If that turbine doesn't go, you die."

He'd left her then, locking the door and
stumping off down the stairs. She'd had all day
and half the night to think about it since, so
the cold wasn't the only thing that was keeping
her from sleep. She paced the dusty boards,
crossing and re-crossing the square of light the
moon cast on her floor, waiting for morning,
yet dreading what the coming day might bring.

CHAPTER 14

BRAINS

"Dad?"

"What is it, Matilda?" It was Friday morning. The Dentons were having breakfast. It had been a quiet meal so far. Titch could see that Mum had been crying again, and there was an irritable edge to her father's voice. The police had done something to the phone and everybody was waiting for it to ring.

"I was thinking about Jill last night."

Her father sighed. "We all were, sweetheart. Nothing's the same without her, is it?"

Titch shook her head, biting her lip to keep from crying. "That's not what I mean though, Dad. I was thinking she can't be far away, because nobody from far away would care about the turbine."

The farmer nodded. "That's what the police

think, Matilda, but it was very cleve
work it out." His wife sniffled and he re
across the table to take her hand.

"And if she's not far away," persisted Titch, "she'll try to get a message to us."

Her father shook his head. "The chap who's holding her will have thought of that, my love. He'll have made sure she can't get a message out."

"Well – that's what I thought too, Dad, but there's more than one sort of message. I know a way she might try to do it."

"Matilda." He smiled gently. "You're a good girl, and I know you only want to help your sister, but this talk is upsetting you mum. Why don't you go and watch TV while we clear away?"

Titch looked at him. "Let me finish, Dad, please. It might be nothing, but I think it's worth thinking about."

Mrs Denton forced a watery smile. "Let her finish, dear – it's all right."

Her husband nodded. "Go on, Matilda."

"Well – this man, whoever he is, will be feeding Jill, won't he?"

"Of course he will. Everybody needs food

and drink."

"Yes," pursued Titch, "and if he's nearby he'll get her food in the village."

"He might," said the farmer, "and he might not. Depends how careful he's being."

Titch pulled a face. "Well, suppose he is getting her stuff in the village? I know what I'd do if I were her."

"What's that, sweetheart?"

Titch looked at him. "What's her favourite drink?"

The farmer smiled sadly. "Cherry cola, and when she comes home I'm going to buy her the biggest bottle I can find."

"Well," said Titch. "If I were Jill, I'd ask this guy for cherry cola every single day. Don't you see?" She looked from her father to her mother and back again. "That'd be a message, wouldn't it? It'd say 'Look – this man's buying a lot of cherry cola all of a sudden, and cherry cola's Jill's favourite drink. Maybe this is the guy who's got Jillo.' "

There was a long silence as Titch's parents gazed at her. It was broken at last by her mother saying, "Matilda, darling, that's absolutely wonderful!" She looked at her husband. "It is an idea, isn't it – one worth following

The farmer nodded slowly. "It's ingenio⌣
he murmured. "The kid puts us all to shame."
He stood up. "I'm off down the shops." He
smiled at his wife. "Your side of the family," he
said. "Must be."

"What's he on about?" frowned Titch, as
her father left the kitchen.

Her mother smiled.

"Brains, darling. Only brains."

CHAPTER 15

MAYBE

He came at exactly half past ten again, masked by his balaclava and dangling a plastic carrier. The only difference was that today he wore a scruffy trench-coat over his black jogging suit. It was drizzling outside and the coat was wet, but he took it off and threw it on Jillo's bed.

"Hey!" Jillo had made up her mind to tread very carefully around her abductor, but the exclamation slipped out before she could stop it. "That coat's dripping, and look where you've put it." She bent down and pulled the coat to the foot of the mattress.

The man didn't answer. He put the bag on the chair and looked at her through his eye-holes. "Bathroom?"

"Please."

Maybe

Back in the attic, Jillo unpacked her food while her kidnapper used a filthy cloth from the bathroom to mop up the puddle that had formed under the broken skylight. When he'd done this, he wrung out the cloth in the fire grate and spread it on the floor to catch drips. "Pity you broke the glass," he sighed. "Better for both of us if you hadn't."

Jillo was sitting on the mattress chewing a cheese and tomato sandwich. A can of Coke stood on the boards between her feet. She nodded towards the can. "Don't like Coke."

The man laughed. "Too bad – we can't always have what we like."

"I don't see why not." She kept her voice soft and low. Mustn't make him angry. "It'd be just as easy for you to get something I like."

"So what do you like, your Majesty?"

"Cherry cola."

"Ugh!" The man shuddered. "You kids – the junk you put inside yourselves!" He chuckled. "Still, why not? Maybe tomorrow it'll be cherry cola."

"Thanks."

"I said maybe." He retrieved the trench-coat, started putting it on. "Got water, have you?"

Jillo nodded. She'd already refilled her can in the bathroom.

"I'll be off then – things to do."

"Have you – spoken to my parents yet?" A dangerous question, but she was desperate to know what was happening. He turned in the doorway. "That's for me to know," he growled.

When he'd gone, Jillo opened her remaining sandwich and scraped off as much of the butter as she could, using a sliver of glass from the grate. She ended up with a dab about the size of a fingernail, which she smeared on a larger piece of glass. Then she squatted by the fireplace and used her scraper to dislodge a clot of ancient soot from the flue. She sprinkled the soot on the butter and used the sliver to mix the two substances into a greasy black paste. She added a few drops of her precious water, stirring the mixture till she had a thickish, oily liquid.

She placed the bit of glass on the chair, taking care not to spill the liquid. Then she knelt by the wall and used her scraper to make a number of incisions in the damp, mildewed wallpaper. By getting her nails into these cuts, she was

able to peel some strips of the paper away from the rotten plaster. These she laid on the floor, pattern side down. Then, using her scraper as a pen and the liquid as ink, she wrote the word HELP on each strip over a crude drawing of a letter O enclosing the figure 5. When all the ink was used up she had seven messages.

She stood under the skylight and poked her hand between the rusty bars. It was still raining. She hid her makeshift tools in the grate and sat down to wait for it to stop.

CHAPTER 16

TAKING THE MICKEY

When Shaz got to the hut at nine that Friday morning the rain was just starting. Mickey and Raider were already there. Shaz peeled off his anorak and draped it over a chair.

"Doesn't look too good."

Mickey glanced out of the window. "No. I reckon it's set for the day. Cuppa tea?"

They sat gazing into their mugs, thinking about Jillo. Raider lapped the tea from his bowl then went and stood in the doorway, watching the rain.

"What we doing today?" asked Shaz.

Mickey shrugged. "I dunno. We've looked everywhere we know. Before you came I started making a list of suspects, but all it is is a list of people I remember from that meeting, with Reuben Kilchaffinch at the top. There were some cranky characters all right, but I don't believe any of 'em would sink to kidnapping."

"We could go down the village," suggested Shaz. "Mooch around."

Mickey nodded. "If you like. It's feeling helpless that gets to you, isn't it? She's out there somewhere needing our help and there's not a thing we can do."

"We're The Outfit," murmured Shaz. "There's got to be something we can do."

It was a quiet morning in Lenton. A few shoppers braved the wet pavements, but the rain had kept most people indoors. It was tempting to imagine that Jillo might be a prisoner in any one of the houses they passed, but they knew the police had made door-to-door inquiries throughout the village.

They'd walked the length of the high street and were passing the churchyard when they saw a familiar figure approaching. Shaz nudged Mickey and whispered, "Pigs can see the wind, you know."

"Shut up," chuckled Mickey. "He might hear you." They straightened their faces as the old man drew near.

"Morning, Postie," smiled Shaz.

"Ah – morning, boys." Postie didn't smile. "I was sorry to hear about your friend. I was talking to her only the other day, you know."

Mickey nodded. "I know, she told us. We just can't believe it."

"There's some wicked folk about these days – not like when I was a lad. We'd a bit of respect in them days."

"When pigs could see the wind, you mean?" Shaz hadn't meant to say it – it just slipped out. The old man looked at him sharply.

"Are you taking the mickey outa me, lad?"

"N – no. No I'm not, Postie. It's just – Jillo said you told her that."

"Aye lad, I did, and it's the truth. When you're my age you'll realize there's some queer things in this world – things your clever scientists know nowt about, with their lasers and quasars and holograms. Anyway." He smiled briefly. "I hope she turns up safe and sound. She seems – hey, what's up with you, boy?"

Raider had returned from an investigation of the churchyard and was taking a great interest in the hem of the old man's raincoat, sniffing and whining.

Mickey flushed. "Raider!" he snapped. "Come away, boy. Sit."

Postie chuckled as Raider settled reluctantly on the shiny pavement. "It's all right," he said. "You get used to dogs when you're a postman. I'll see you later, then – and I hope the little lass'll be with you when I do."

Mickey nodded. "So do we. See you, Postie! C'mon Raider."

Raider gazed after the old postman for a moment, then got up and followed the boys.

CHAPTER 17

AS FAR AS WE DARE

Mum was in the bathroom and Dad hadn't got back yet, so it was Titch who picked up the phone.

"Lenton 4686."

"Is your daddy there?"

"No, he's out. Who is this?"

"Never mind. Is your mummy there?"

"She's upstairs. Can I take a message or get her to ring you back?"

"Here's the message. If the turbine's still in one piece Monday night, the kid dies."

"It's you!" gasped Titch. "You let my sister go, you cruel, horrible—"

She heard the click as the caller rang off. She was still holding the receiver when her mother came into the room. "Who – was it him, darling?" Titch nodded, replacing the receiver.

"What did he say?"

"He said if the turbine's still in one piece Monday night, the kid dies."

"Oh my God! Then that's it. The minute your dad gets back he must—" Mrs Denton glanced at the clock. "Where is he, for heaven's sake?"

As she spoke the door opened and a uniformed sergeant poked his head round. "Sorry, Mrs Denton," he said. "It was a callbox, but he rang off before we could complete the trace."

The woman shook her head. "It doesn't matter. We're going to do what he wants."

The sergeant shook his head. "I – my inspector doesn't think that would be a good idea, Mrs Denton. Not at this stage, when we've every hope of—"

"Sergeant." The woman's voice was unsteady. "It's my daughter's life we're talking about. I don't care if the turbine goes and you never catch this man, just as long as my child comes home unharmed."

The officer nodded. "I can understand that of course, Mrs Denton. If it were my daughter I'd feel exactly—"

There were footfalls in the hallway and the sergeant stepped aside to let the farmer enter the room. He looked around. "What's going on?"

Briefly, his wife told him about the phone call and the kidnapper's ultimatum. "The sergeant here thinks we should wait," she said, "but I want that turbine down. I want the work to start today, so that whoever is holding Jill can see we're doing what he wants. I want my child back."

The farmer nodded, folding his wife in his arms. "You're right," he soothed. "We're not going to gamble with Jill's life for the sake of a blessed piece of machinery." He looked across at the policeman. "I'm sorry, Sergeant – we've cooperated as far as we dare, but now I'm going to phone the contractor – explain the situation and get him to come and start dismantling the turbine." He shook his head. "I wish I'd never set eyes on the damn thing."

Titch went up to her room and stood at the window, looking towards the turbine. Its shape was blurred and softened by the rain. She wondered whether Jillo's kidnapper was looking at it too. Where was he? Who was he?

Would they ever know, now that the turbine was coming down? "I'm like Mum," she whispered. "I don't care, if only Jillo comes home safe and well."

CHAPTER 18

SOME KID

Jillo was nibbling the last bit of her sandwich and sipping water from the can when she noticed it had stopped raining. She looked at her watch. Two o'clock. She lifted a corner of the mattress and took out her seven messages. She stood under the skylight and stuck her hand between the bars, testing the breeze. It was fairly strong. She took the first message, kissed it, and held it up. The wind plucked it from her fingers. She saw it for an instant as it rose, spinning, and then it was gone. She imagined it flying over trees and meadows to Denton Farm, floating down like a snowflake on to the grass outside the hut where her friends would find it.

And then what? With a sinking feeling, she realized her message would convey very little. She'd written the word help, but how could they help if they'd no idea where she was? And how could she tell them where she was when she didn't know?

She sat on the chair, holding the six remaining messages, thinking. She could put old house, but there are old houses everywhere. Derelict house would be better, but it was too long – she hadn't much ink. Empty house, then? She remembered the canal. Empty house by the canal. It was long, but quite useful if they were searching for her. She imagined herself as a stranger, finding such a message. What would she do? She'd wonder who'd written it, wouldn't she? And why? Was it somebody having a joke? Some kid? Probably. After all, you just don't find messages like this in real life. My name – it should have my name on it. My name's bound to have been in the paper and on telly. Missing girl. Everybody will have seen it. If I put my name, even a stranger will know who wrote it.

She retrieved her bits of glass from the grate and set to work. She thinned the ink with spit, but even so it ran out halfway through the third message. She laid aside her makeshift pen and looked at the two she'd completed.

HELP. EMPTY HOUSE NEAR CANAL. JILL DENTON. And then of course there was The Outfit badge, which would mean nothing to a stranger.

She carried the two scraps of wallpaper to the skylight and released them. She knew the chances were that they'd fall into thickets or hedge bottoms or long grass where they'd never be found. They could even end up in the canal where her ink would wash out, but at least she was doing something to help herself. Better than just sitting here, waiting to see whether her mad captor would really...

She shook her head to dispel unwanted thoughts, and looked around for something else to do.

CHAPTER 19

CHERRY COLA

"There y'are, your Highness – cherry cola."
He sounds chipper, thought Jillo, catching the
carrier he swung towards her. Even through
that spooky balaclava.

"And look." He held up the raincoat.
"Dry, okay?" He dropped it on the mattress.
"Bathroom, your Majesty?"

She could hear him on the landing as she
washed, walking to and fro, humming a tune.
He sounded so cheerful that halfway up the
stairs she risked a question. "Has something
good happened?"

"Oh, yes. Something good has happened.
Something very good, for me and for you."

"What is it?"

He chuckled. "Wouldn't you like to know?"

"Well, yes – of course I would. That's why I

asked."

"Well then, I'll tell you. The turbine's coming down."

"It is?" Her heart kicked. She felt a huge weight lift off her shoulders. She was trembling so much her legs wobbled and she dropped on to the chair, surprised by the tears which filled her eyes. "Does that mean you'll – that I can go home?"

There was no reply. The man had his back to her. He seemed to be looking at something. She dashed the tears away as he turned.

"What's the paper for?" His voice was muffled as always, but there was no mistaking the menace in it.

"What paper?"

"The paper from the wall."

She gulped, then shook her head. "I don't know what you mean."

"OH YES YOU DO!" It was a screech. "YOU TORE PAPER FROM THE WALL – THERE!" He jabbed a finger towards the bare plaster. "WHAT'S IT FOR??"

"M-messages," stammered Jillo. "But it doesn't matter now, does it?"

"DOESN'T MATTER? OF COURSE IT

MATTERS!" He strode forward, grabbed her by the shoulders and shook her so violently her teeth chattered. "WHERE ARE THEY, THESE MESSAGES? WHAT HAVE YOU DONE WITH THEM?"

"The w-w-window," she gasped. "Out the window."

"Out the window." His voice dropped. The shaking stopped, but his nails still bit into her flesh. "And what was in these messages, eh? What did you tell 'em?" She could see his eyes, burning out at her through the knitted mask.

"N-nothing. My name. Where I am. The word help. That's all."

"You're lying. They were about the ray gun, weren't they?"

"No!" She shook her head.

"Oh yes they were!" He dug his nails in. "I know what you told 'em. I'm not stupid. You told 'em to move the ray gun, didn't you?"

"No!"

"Yes you did. Take down the turbine, you said, but move the ray gun. Put it in the pylon. He won't know. BUT I DO!" He flung her from him so violently that the chair went over backwards and Jillo struck her head on the floor. She lay dazed as her captor ranted on, his voice seeming to come from a great distance. I know, it said. You thought to trick me, but I know. I can feel the rays, just like before.

She must have passed out then, because the next thing she knew, she was lying on the mattress and her captor had gone. His voice was still there though, raving insider her head, and everywhere she looked she saw those mad, gleaming eyes. When she recalled how her heart had soared when he told her his news, she rolled over, buried her face in the blanket and wept.

CHAPTER 20

CRACK

When the workmen broke for lunch the tower was nothing but a stump in the middle of the field. Its blades, motor and top sections lay in two trucks which stood by the field gate. Mickey, Shaz and Raider watched from a distance as the four men settled down in the gateway, producing flasks and packets of sandwiches. Only Mr Denton remained by the stump. He stood with his hands in his pockets, gazing at the remains of his turbine.

"Let's go over," suggested Shaz. "Ask if he's heard anything."

Mickey shook his head. "I dunno, Shaz. It's a rotten time for him, waiting. He might not want company."

"Hmmm," murmured Shaz. "Maybe not. I wish we'd cracked it, Mickey – The Outfit, I mean. Rescued Jillo and brought the kidnapper to justice. It feels like we've let her down when it really matters, doesn't it?"

Mickey nodded. "Mind you, it won't matter as long as he keeps his promise. Just think – she could show up at any minute."

"I know. I wish she would."

Titch sat at the kitchen table. Her mother was looking out of the window. After a moment she left the room and went to the front door, which had stood open all morning. She remained there for a minute then came back to the kitchen, looking at her watch and out of the window. Titch said, "She'll come soon, Mum – you'll see."

Her mother shook her head. "I hope so, darling. If she doesn't I think I'll lose my mind."

The phone rang. Titch and her mother looked at it, then at each other. "Aren't you going to get it?" murmured Titch.

The woman nodded, crossed the room and snatched up the receiver.

"Hello?" Titch sat twisting her fingers together, listening.

"What – what d'you mean? What ray gun?

What are you talking about?" Titch saw the colour drain from her mother's face. She stood up.

"What?" The woman's voice cracked. "We can't do that – you know we can't. It's not our pylon. You said – we've dismantled the turbine. You promised ... hello?"

Titch stared as her mother replaced the receiver. "Wh-what is it, Mum? What did he say?"

The woman shook her head. "Never mind. Fetch Daddy, please. Quickly now."

In the cellar, the constable shrugged. "No go, Sarge. Doesn't stay on long enough."

The sergeant shook his head. "Nutter though, isn't he? Out and out nutter, capable of anything. I pity that poor kid, and the parents. I'd go barmy if she was mine."

The constable nodded. "The lads'll find him, Sarge. Just a matter of time."

"Time." The sergeant sighed. "I've a feeling time's the stuff we're running out of, son. I've seen these nuts before. They hold themselves together for just so long, then something happens and they crack." He shook his head.

"I wouldn't want a kid of mine in this feller's way when that happens."

CHAPTER 21

ALMOST TOMORROW

He's never going to let me go. Jillo was sitting on the mattress, huddled in her blankets. It was eleven o'clock on Saturday night and the attic was so cold she could see her breath by the faint light of the stars. He's never going to let me go. That's one of the bad things. The other bad things are, I'm cold, it's dark, I'm by myself, and I don't know how it's all going to end. Are there any good things?

Well, yes. Lots of them. I'm alive for a start. I'm not tied up – I can walk about. I've got a good brain so I can make plans. He comes only once a day, so there's time to try things out. I'm part of The Outfit so the others will be looking for me. And – she smiled briefly – he's passing on my cherry cola message without knowing it, so he's not as smart as he thinks he is.

Okay – what have I done, what am I doing and what else can I try? I've written messages and posted them through the window. Two messages. They're out there somewhere unless he's found them. I daren't do any more because he'd notice if more wallpaper disappeared.

I've shouted to Raider, but I don't think that did any good. I've tried getting out, but the door's solid and the skylight's barred.

I'm sending the cherry cola message, but it'll be a few days before anyone notices, even if they're looking.

And that's it, up to now. There's got to be something else I can do.

The floor! If there's a loose floorboard somewhere, maybe I could break through into the room below. Not now. Too dark. In the morning then, straight after his visit.

Anything else?

She sat, watching the plumes of her breath, thinking.

His visits. There must be some way I can use his visits. What happens? Let's go through it, step by step. He comes up the stairs and unlocks the door. I'm standing in the middle of the room, dying to go to the toilet. That's what he expects. But what if I charged at him before he knew what was happening? Could I get past him? Down two flights? Would the door be locked, and if it was, could I smash my way through a window? He doesn't move so fast – I bet I could outrun him easy. She nodded. Could be worth a try if things get desperate – better than just waiting for him to…

What happens next? He comes in, puts the carrier bag on the chair and throws his coat on the bed. The door's always open, but he always keeps himself between me and the door. Then we go down to the bathroom, but he goes first so I can't run. Suppose I shoved him in the back, really hard, when we were still near the top of the stairs? Would he crash down the whole flight? Would the fall stun him so I could get past? She grinned. Maybe he'd break his neck.

So then I'm in the bathroom, but the window's boarded up and he's right outside. Nothing there. We go back up, me first. I unpack the carrier, he looks out the skylight or prowls round the room. The door's unlocked, but I suppose he's ready if I try to make a dash. The carrier. Could I slip something into the carrier? She shook her head. Nobody'd see it but him, you div! It might be different if I could pin something to the outside of the carrier without him noticing, but there's no chance. He puts yesterday's can and sandwich wrapper in the carrier, gets his coat from the bed and...

Just a minute! She caught her breath. His coat. She'd sat on the mattress with the coat beside her, nibbling her sandwich. Suppose...? Her heart kicked. Yes! It could work. If I've got the stuff ready and he looks out the skylight as he usually does, it might be possible. I'm going to try it anyway. I am. I am. She looked at her watch. It was two minutes to midnight.

Almost tomorrow.

CHAPTER 22

BADGE

He came at nine o'clock, dumping the carrier on the chair and his coat on the bed as usual.

"You're early," ventured Jillo on the stairs. She hadn't had time to check the floorboards.

The balaclava nodded. "Sunday. No shopping. Did it yesterday."

"Ah."

It was cherry cola again. She opened it and sat on the mattress, sipping from the can. He scrutinized the wallpaper, then stood looking through the skylight.

The badge was under a blanket. Stealthily, watching him all the time, she drew it out. Her heart was pounding but she forced herself to move slowly. Resting a hand casually on the coat, she drew it towards her, pinned the badge in the middle of the back and turned the garment so it was hidden.

The next ten minutes were the longest of Jillo's life, but when it was time for him to go he picked up the coat and shrugged into it without noticing anything amiss. "Tomorrow," he grunted in the doorway. Jillo nodded, straight-faced. Not if The Outfit spots that badge, she thought.

CHAPTER 23
CLEVER, THAT

"Morning boys!" Mickey and Shaz were sitting on a wooden seat in the sunshine, watching the people go into church. They looked up. Postie's smile was sympathetic. "Still no word about your friend, then?"

Mickey shook his head. "Not yet. We're following a lead, though."

"Oh, yes – what sort of a lead?"

Mickey smiled wryly. "We are looking for someone who's buying a lot of cherry cola."

"Cherry…" The old man stared. "What d'you mean? Why cherry cola, for goodness' sake?"

Mickey shrugged. "Jillo's favourite drink. Her dad says if someone's buying cherry cola who doesn't usually, that could be our man."

"I see. Yes, Clever, that. I'd never have

thought of it. Well – I'll be getting along. See you later."

The boys nodded. "See you, Postie." He started to move away, and it was then that Shaz saw the badge on the back of his coat.

CHAPTER 24

OLD COUNTRY TALES

"D'you think – d'you think this man could have something to do with pigs?"

Sunday morning, nine-thirty. The Dentons at their sad and jumpy breakfast. The farmer looked across the table at his drained, tearful wife. "A pig farmer, you mean?"

"Yes, or someone who works for one. I just wondered, because it was such an odd thing for somebody to say."

The farmer nodded. "Yes, it was. I'll mention it to the inspector if you like, but I doubt if it's significant. It sounds like one of these old country tales to me."

Pigs. Titch was playing with her cornflakes, building a castle with a moat of milk. She seldom spoke at breakfast these days, because a word would sometimes trigger an angry outburst or a flood of tears. Pigs, though. She looked up. "What did he say, Mum?"

Her mother shook her head. "It was nothing, darling. Just a saying of some sort."

"About pigs?"

"Matilda." Her father gave her a look that meant don't bother your mother – she's upset enough as it is.

Titch looked down and her mother said, "Yes dear, it was about pigs. He said, 'I can see those rays like pigs can see the wind.'"

Titch froze with the spoon halfway to her mouth. A thread of milk dribbled into her bowl. Her father frowned at her. "What is it, Matilda? You look as if you've seen a ghost."

Titch lowered the spoon, spilling more milk because her hand was trembling. "It's not a ghost, Dad," she croaked. "I think I know who's got Jill."

CHAPTER 25

GOODBYE, PLEASE

"Mickey!" Shaz grabbed his friend's sleeve.

"What?"

"D'you see it – on his coat?"

"What on his coat? What you on about, Shaz?"

"Look." Shaz pointed. "On Postie's coat – an Outfit badge!"

"Don't talk wet!" Mickey screwed up his eyes. "I can see something on his coat, but it can't be an Outfit badge, unless Titch lost hers and he found it."

"If he found it," cried Shaz, "why the heck would he stick it on the back of his coat, you div? It's Jillo's badge, Mickey – she put it there. He's got her!"

"What, old Postie? Never."

"He must have. He was interested in the

cherry cola lead, wasn't he?"

"I didn't notice."

"Well, he was. And he seems in a bit of a rush, too. I bet if we follow him home we'll find Jillo. Come on."

Postie's cottage was in Yew Tree Lane, behind the church. As soon as the old man passed from sight the boys got up and followed. When they turned into the lane he was by his front door, fishing in his pocket. They flattened themselves against a wall and watched as he produced a latchkey, let himself in and closed the door. Mickey looked at Shaz. "Now what?"

Shaz pulled a face. "We knock, and when he answers we say we've come for Jillo. He'll be so startled he'll give himself away. Then we shove him aside and get her."

Mickey shook his head. "I don't fancy it, Shaz. Mr Denton reckons the kidnapper's a madman. Don't you think it's a job for the police?"

"No, I don't," said Shaz. "I think it's a job for The Outfit. You were saying we felt like we'd let Jillo down. Well, here's our chance to make up for it."

Mickey hesitated for a moment, then nodded. "Okay, only I wish Raider was here."

A short path bisected Postie's tiny garden. The pair walked up it and Shaz knocked loudly on the door. It swung open almost at once. Postie was in his stockinged feet. He smiled. "What can I do for you, boys?"

"We've come for Jillo," said Shaz.

Mickey was ready to leap forward if the old man tried to slam the door, but he didn't. Instead he smiled ruefully and said, "So. The game's up, as they say. I suspected it might be when I found this on my coat just now." He showed them Jillo's badge. "You'd better come in."

The doorway opened straight into the front room. As Mickey and Shaz stepped inside, the old man closed the door, picked up the shotgun he'd concealed behind it and levelled it at them.

"I'm sorry, boys," he smiled. "I wouldn't normally shoot children but you see it's the rays. They made me take your friend, and now it's come to this. Say goodbye, please."

CHAPTER 26

WALKIES

"You can't," breathed Mickey. "You'd go to jail for ever."

The old man yapped a laugh but the gun didn't waver. "Goodbye, boys." They saw his finger begin to squeeze the trigger. Mickey felt for his friend's hand. They closed their eyes.

"Albert!" At the sound of his name the old man spun round. The door burst open, catching the end of the gun barrel, knocking it aside. The boys opened their eyes in time to see Farmer Denton fling himself on Postie. Both men crashed to the floor, wrestling for possession of the gun. "Run, boys!" gasped the farmer. "Go on – get out of here!"

"Come on, Shaz." Mickey skirted the heaving men and ran into the garden with Shaz at his heels. Looking back, they saw that the farmer had snatched up the gun and was getting up. They watched through the doorway as he backed the snarling madman into a corner.

"Where's my daughter?" he rapped. "What have you done with her?"

"She's not here," spat Postie. "You can do what you like with me but I'll never tell where she is." He laughed. "She'll starve to death while you search."

"What's happening – where's Jill?" The boys turned to see Mrs Denton coming through the gateway.

Mickey shook his head. "Mr Denton's got Postie, but he says Jill's not here."

"Then where – where is she? If he's harmed her..." She pushed past Mickey.

As she reached the doorway a siren wailed and a police van screeched to a stop by the gate. Three men piled out and ran up the path. They brushed the two boys aside and went through the doorway.

"All right, sir," said the sergeant, taking the gun from the farmer. "We'll look after this gentleman now." He looked at the old man. "Will you walk out, or do we have to carry you?"

"I've walked up and down garden paths all my life," snarled Postie. "I can walk down my own, but you'll never find the kid."

Mickey and Shaz watched as they led the old man away. One policeman stayed in the house. The Dentons came out.

"What were you two doing here?" asked the farmer. Mickey told him about the badge. Denton nodded. "A message from Jill." His wife stifled a sob.

"How about you?" asked Shaz. "If you hadn't shown up when you did, we'd both be dead now."

"That was Matilda. She remembered something that old lunatic said about pigs."

"Pigs can see the wind?"

"That's it. I couldn't really believe it was old Albert till I looked through that window and saw him with the gun."

"What'll happen now?" asked Mickey.

The farmer shrugged. "The police'll work on him – make him tell where Jill is." He put his arm round his wife's shoulders. "Come on, love – we'll wait at the police station."

The boys watched as the couple walked

slowly to their car. Titch was in the back seat. She waved to Shaz and Mickey. They waved back. The car was driven away.

"Well," sighed Shaz. "That was a bit too exciting – I'm shaking like jelly."

Mickey nodded. "Me too, and we haven't finished yet."

Shaz looked at him. "But surely we can only wait now, like the Dentons?"

Mickey shook his head. "No way, Shaz old son. Let others sit and wait – The Outfit's going walkies."

CHAPTER 27

CROWDED HOTELS

Raider heard them coming and yipped excitedly. Mickey grinned. "He sounds keen – it just might work." He unlocked the caravan door and the dog jumped up to lick his face.

"Gerroff, you sloppy mutt! Listen." He grabbed Raider's forepaws and gazed into his eyes. "Jillo, right? You remember Jillo, don't you?"

"Yip!" Moonlight on water. A big old house.

"Good," said Mickey, "because we want you to find her. Find Jillo, boy – go find Jillo."

Shaz laughed. "You're crazy, Mickey, d'you know that? You think that dog's human."

"I do not!" retorted Mickey. "I think he's superhuman." He turned back to Raider. "Jillo – go get Jillo." He let go of the dog's paws. Raider dropped on to all fours and trotted

97

about, whining and sniffing the grass.

Shaz laughed again. "Superhuman? Look at him – he hasn't a clue."

"Give him a chance, " protested Mickey. "Sunday's his day off. Hey, Raider – Jillo. Go find Jillo."

Raider yipped. He recognized the name. He could even see a dim picture of Jillo inside his head, and her scent clung faintly to the badge on his collar. Trouble was, it was all mixed up with something else – somewhere he'd been once, at night, near water. A place with a bad feel to it. Something to do with a dark old house.

"Jillo," cried Mickey. "Go get Jillo."

A stile. Raider stopped sniffing and whined, looking towards the farm. He'd found something near a stile. A scent. That's how it had begun. And he knew that stile – of course he did. He yipped and set off towards the twenty-acre.

"Yeee-haaaa!" whooped Mickey. "Here we go, Shaz." He set off after the dog, singing "Here we go, here we go, here we go," like a soccer fan. Shaz slammed the caravan door and followed.

Raider didn't look back. He crossed the twenty-acre to the stile, picked up the scent and set off south-east. Mickey yelled over his shoulder to Shaz, "The wood – he's heading for Weeping Wood."

Shaz caught up with Mickey in the middle of the wood. "Where the heck's he taking us?" he gasped.

Mickey shook his head.

"Dunno, but *he* seems to. All we can do is follow."

They ran on. Raider was mostly out of sight now, but he barked from time to time to give them his direction. Presently the trees thinned and the boys saw the glint of water ahead.

"It's the old canal," panted Shaz. "Surely Postie can't have dragged her this far?"

"Why not? He's a pretty fit guy from a lifetime's walking, and the further from Lenton the better, I suppose, from his point of view."

"Maybe," grunted Shaz. "I just hope that mutt of yours isn't leading us on a wild goose chase."

There was a high wall now, on their left. Halfway along it stood Raider, barking and watching their approach. As they came up to him they saw ivy-smothered gateposts and a house half hidden by trees.

They stopped.

"What place is this?" asked Shaz. He stood bent over, hands on knees, panting.

Mickey shrugged, dashing sweat from his forehead with the back of his hand. "Dunno. I've never been this way. Looks empty."

"Yes, well it would be, wouldn't it?" scoffed Shaz. "Kidnappers don't usually put their victims in crowded hotels. We going in or what?" Raider, standing between the gateposts wagging his tail and looking at them, seemed to be asking the same question.

" 'Course we're going in," cried Mickey. "We're The Outfit."

CHAPTER 28

LIVING TO BE TEN

Jillo had two floorboards up and was kicking a hole in the lath and plaster when she heard footfalls on the stairs. Thinking her abductor had returned, she grabbed the boards she'd ripped up and began fitting them back in place, praying he wouldn't reach the attic till she'd finished. She'd got the first one down and was slotting in the second when she heard a volley of barks and a frantic scrabbling at the door.

"Raider!" She leapt up and ran to the door, pressing her palms and her ear to it. "How'd you get in, boy? Where's Mickey?"

Raider whined and barked, and then all at once she heard feet on the stairs and a familiar voice yelled, "Okay, Jillo – The Outfit's here!"

"Mickey!" Jillo rattled the doorknob. "I'm in here. It's locked."

"Not for long," cried a second voice, and Jillo called out, "Hurry, Shaz, please – he's mad. He senses things. He'll come."

"No, he won't," laughed Shaz. "The police have got him. Stand away from the door."

She backed off. There was a series of heavy thumps, which made the door shudder and knocked showers of dust and plaster from around its frame. At the fifth thump, the wood near the ancient lock began to crack. "It's going!" cried Jillo. The next blow splintered it, and the seventh tore the lock from its housing so that the boys hurtled into the room off balance and fell in a heap on the floor. Sobbing with thankfulness and relief, Jillo threw herself on top of them and the trio laughed and cried and hugged while Raider ran round them, yipping and growling.

It was some time before Mickey disentangled himself from the mêlée and stood up, knocking dust off his jeans. "Hey," he gasped. "Your folks'll be frantic, Jillo – they don't even know you're safe yet."

Jillo sat up and wiped her cheeks with her hands, leaving smudges of dust like war paint. "You're right," she sniffled. "We're being thoughtless." She smiled. "It's just so wonderful – so unbelievable to be free." She stood up, grabbed Shaz's hand and hauled him to his feet.

They walked out of the attic, dusting themselves down. In the doorway, Jillo looked back at the mattress, the fireplace, the spindly chair. A lifetime seemed to have passed since she saw these things for the first time.

Mickey turned on the stairs. "What's up – going to miss the place, are you?"

Jillo shook her head. "No, but I'll never forget it, Mickey. Not if I live to be a hundred." She felt her heart lift. "An hour ago," she smiled, "I'd have settled for living to be ten."

CHAPTER 29

YIP!

Saturday morning. A week had gone by since Jillo's rescue. Titch and the boys had been to school, but the Dentons had kept Jillo at home to recover from her ordeal. Today was the first time the two girls had been allowed to come to the hut, and now Raider and the four children sat round the table, talking.

"What'll happen to Postie?" wondered Shaz. Jillo pulled a face.

"I didn't believe it when you told me it was old Postie under that balaclava. He looked so scary – those eyes!"

"Dad says he couldn't help what he did," said Titch. "His mind's sick. They'll send him somewhere for treatment – a hospital that's a sort of prison, too."

Yip!

"I hope they can cure him," murmured Shaz. "He was okay, old Postie."

Mickey looked at Jillo. "Will your folks rebuild the turbine?"

Jillo shrugged. "They haven't decided." She smiled. "I think Dad's reluctant to hurt the protest group after the way they all turned out to search for me."

"Did they?"

"Yes – even old Reuben."

"I loved the bit Linda Fellgate put in the paper about us," chuckled Shaz. "And the way she let us wear our badges for the picture. I vote we have it on the wall."

"It'll be on the wall all right," said Jillo. "Mum's sent for the original – the glossy. She's having it professionally framed for us. It's a sort of thank you to The Outfit."

Talking about The Outfit," said Titch, "isn't it about time—"

"WE DID THE OATH!" shouted the others in unison. Chairs scraped back as the children left the table and formed a circle, holding hands. Raider stood in the middle with his tongue hanging out and his tail wagging. They squatted.

"Faithful, fearless, full of fun,
Winter, summer, rain or sun,
One for five and five for one –
THE OUTFIT!"

They shouted the last line and leapt upright, arms held high.

"Yip!" went Raider, and the circle broke in laughter as he snuffled Jillo's leg. She was back. They were together. Everything was fine.

READ ALL OF THE OUTFIT'S THRILLING ADVENTURES!

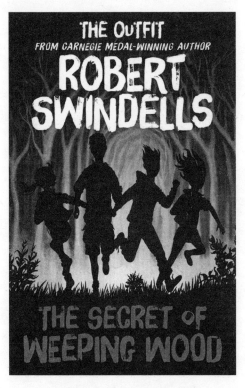

ISBN 978-1-78270-053-1

The Outfit had never really believed
the stories about the ghosts of Weeping
Wood – until now. But as they investigate
the mysterious cries, truth suddenly
becomes stranger – and more
terrifying – than fiction!

READ ALL OF THE OUTFIT'S THRILLING ADVENTURES!

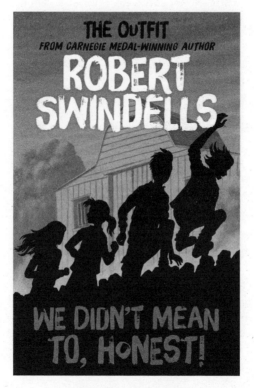

ISBN 978-1-78270-054-8

Miserable Reuben Kilchaffinch is going
to fill in Froglet Pond, and he won't let
anything, or anyone, get in his way.
The Outfit are desperate to save the pond
and its wildlife and they plan to stop
Kilchaffinch – at any cost!

READ ALL OF THE OUTFIT'S THRILLING ADVENTURES!

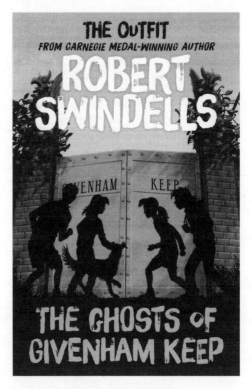

THE OUTFIT
FROM CARNEGIE MEDAL-WINNING AUTHOR
ROBERT SWINDELLS

GIVENHAM KEEP

THE GHOSTS OF GIVENHAM KEEP

ISBN 978-1-78270-056-2

Steel gates and barbed wire have
been put up around the old mansion in
Weeping Wood. Someone has something to
hide and The Outfit intend to find out what.
But their innocent investigation soon
takes a sinister turn...

READ ALL OF THE OUTFIT'S THRILLING ADVENTURES!

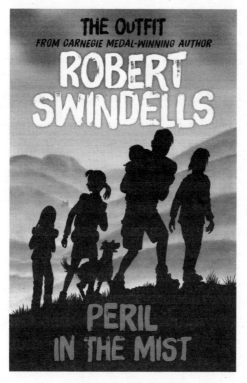

ISBN 978-1-78270-057-9

A challenging hike across five remote moors
is just the sort of adventure The Outfit love.
But when they find themselves alone on the
moors as mist descends and night falls,
will The Outfit be able to overcome
their greatest challenge yet?

READ ALL OF THE OUTFIT'S THRILLING ADVENTURES!

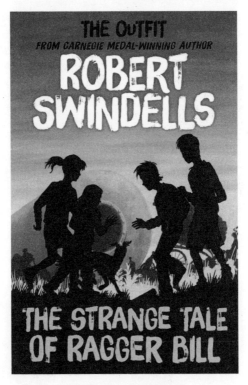

ISBN 978-1-78270-058-6

A little girl has gone missing and some of the villagers are taking matters into their own hands. Ragger Bill is the main suspect, but The Outfit are sure he is innocent. They must find the true culprit – and fast – before things go too far!